Rebecca
Why Did She Run?

by Martha Wiley

Illustrations by Michelle Mirakian

Mow Tomorrow Books, LLC

With special thanks to Karen Osborne, a master encourager!

This is a work of historical fiction. Rebecca, her children, Sam Turner, and John Spencer (Sir John) were actual people, but names for other people were invented. Many of the episodes have been related over the years by family but are given context in this story. The epilogue explains this further.

Mow Tomorrow Books, LLC

Second Edition
ISBN: 979-8-9901272-9-6
Text Copyright © 2026 Martha Wiley
Illustrations and Cover Design Copyright © 2025 Michelle Mirakian

First Installment

This isn't the way it was supposed to turn out. Life with John and all those people who looked so shiny and perfect was supposed to make her grand. It was supposed to be like Cinderella. She was a poor girl lifted up by her prince-charming to a life as a princess. People would love her. Anybody who underestimated her would see they were wrong. Little Rebecca could make up her own mind and make things happen. She would be lovely, remarkable, and strong. At least that is how he made her feel. Virginia was a new land where proud Englishmen of means could make their fortune, and she was chosen to be part of that. People who had their roots as aristocrats could become wealthy and build their own royalty. She thought this was what she wanted, but she was so wrong.

Her family had their roots in England too and looked to the new world as a land of opportunity. They had skills and aimed to grow a family with new soil, lush green hills, and sparkling water. They weren't the fancy level, but if you were smart, there was no telling how happy you could be. Besides, some of those guys who thought they were so smart didn't have what it takes to hold onto what they had.

Her daddy and mama saw Trip starting to hang around their daughter Rebecca when he came over to get supplies and trade for horses with his papa, Sir Spencer. The visits became more frequent. Even though she was just a young teenager, she seemed much older. She had command of the young ones, and they followed her lead happily. It was like she had just the right touch.

Trip was a good deal older and a bit of a rebel and dreamer. This didn't suit his folks at home. He was actually Trip, short for John R. Spencer III.

His father was John Spencer II. People wondered how he would do as master of a plantation. He didn't have the same shrewd drive as Old Sir John. Rebecca was a marvel to him with a fire inside that reminded him of horses pulling in first at the races. She would make his father proud. She was much like Old Sir John's first wife. After she died, the current wife would never measure up, and everybody knew it.

When the Akers family was told of the intention of this bright-eyed couple, Daddy thought it was wonderful. Having a blood tie to the Spencer farm could do nothing but help his business. Rebecca was his gem. Of course they would treat her right.

Mama was not so sure. "Girl, they're not like us. They will look down on you. You won't be able to do anything right. They will always be better. They are not always nice. Can you change? They won't care what you think is right.

Oh! why hadn't she listened more to Mama?

The tears never seemed to stop now. She looked in the mirror and saw the start of a tired old woman, even though she was barely in her twenties. She wasn't able to raise her children the way she wanted. She was continually being corrected and shoved aside. Her wonderful husband was no longer there, and it was obvious some of the others wanted her to leave and wanted her children gone too. She wasn't really going to be "The Lady Spencer." Others were angling for that position and knew how to do it. And here was Mr. Turner. He could be her way out. But she would have to run for it. The two little ones would have to stay behind, but she could take the two older boys. The nanny loved all her kids. She was the one person in the house that Rebecca could trust.

As she thought back to her first ride into the big house it seemed like that was another world away. Maybe they hadn't started the right way. Maybe she was part of the problem.

* * *

She sat tall and stroked the neck of Ginger as she rode up the circular drive heading toward the group gathered on a front porch. She could feel the horse's pulse, matching her own as she rode toward her new life. Daddy rode beside her on the right and Trip was in front, on a thoroughbred that the Spencers bought from her family a few years back. Behind came another horse that carried her few belongings. This animal was a gift for the Old Sir John.

Her home had been hill country where the entire family worked the crops and tended the stock. Daddy was known for his horses. Big planters like Old Sir John came in to pick the best that would work hard in the field and run hard at the track. Bragging rights for a powerful showing at the races meant a lot. They shopped for spirit and strength, and Daddy knew how to deliver. He seemed to know a lot of secrets that brought out the very best. All the neighbors admired what he could produce. They would come for vegetables, rye whiskey, and horses. They would laugh, tell stories, and drive a bargain.

Ginger was hers, and they were out to the bean patch with the little kids when she first met Trip. Rebecca ran her enthusiastic crew for the harvest. She had a way of making them feel important, proud to be part of the family, singing those church-going songs while the little fingers dropped bean pods into baskets. They knew they could trust her to take care of their needs and heap on appreciation and encouragement. She made it like a game with plenty of play. When their work was complete, she would line them along Ginger's back while she led the parade back home. Then they would start the going home song in loud chorus. Mama could hear them coming through the valley and know they were on the way.

Trip heard it too when he was out horse-buying with his dad. He would love to have a family like this. He could tell that Mr. Akers didn't just have a knack for horses. There was something about his kids as well. Trip's home was nothing like this hill country brood. His temperament made him feel like a misfit in the big house. A young man was quick to be shamed, honor was paramount, and the competition was fierce. He knew he was the oldest son, and expectations weighed heavily on him. He was the only child for Old Sir John's first wife. When she died in childbirth, there were other wives, then there were a lot of baby girls before finally a little boy. The patriarch wanted a man in his direct line. The girls would all marry and not be Spencers anymore. How could the glorious plantation he had worked so hard to build not carry his family name down to next generations. He had over 100 slaves to work the fields and take care of the house. From the battle of Hastings on down, his people had the respect and advantage that assured them a position. This importance was part of who they were.

Rebecca edged her mare over closer to her father and dipped her chin. "Daddy?"

"It will be OK. They are going to love you. You and Trip will have lots of sons. That's just what they want." Daddy was sure that she held the key to the future for both families.

"But they wanted us to wait on that bishop from Jamaica. An uncle something or other. We aren't Anglicans, Daddy. Trip wanted to be married right away, and Rev. Walker was passing through on his circuit. It was an honest church wedding. I didn't know it was that important to them."

Her father chuckled and said, "Maybe you should have waited until you were done scrubbing the floor. Shoes would have been nice."

"I wish they would just forget about that. We are married!" With a deep breath she lifted her head.

Daddy said, "This is your home now. Look at it. Won't be the hard to get used to."

She scanned the big house that had room for many families and a full staff of folks to clean and serve and cook. The procession was going slowly down the tree-lined approach. Cabins for slaves were off down the side. The barns were full of horses and cattle. There were especially nice stables for some of the horses and corrals for exercise. Groomsmen were out with regal steeds held by bridles to the east of the porch.

Reading the faces on the porch was tough. Old Sir John was easy to spot. He'd been to the Akers' house every season. The other older men were probably his brothers or neighbors. Somewhere in the black faces was the girl that Trip said was for her and for when they had their own children. The woman standing in front of the others might John's stepmother, the current Lady Spencer. She held a boy just about toddler age. Other children were mixed around the legs of adults. Who were cousins, and who were stepsisters and brothers? What were they expecting to see?

Trip looked marvelous as he moved into a trot up to the porch, came to a stop, swung a leg over and hit the ground. In just a few strides he was on the steps and going toward his father. "Sir, I'm here to present Mrs. John R. Spencer the third. She will now be part of our family."

At that, he turned, walked quickly back to Ginger holding his arms up to Rebecca, showing that she should let him lift her down. She and Ginger always worked together, and this dismount was new. She didn't need help, but that had to be part of some ceremony. Daddy landed quietly on the ground and took her bundle from the back of the last horse. His hand rested briefly on her shoulder "You'll be fine."

Old Sir John looked on her kindly and said, "Jenny, show your new mistress to her room and take her things."

An older girl stepped forward, this was all new. Mistress now? Someone else to carry? Where was this room? All for her? This clearly wasn't like the life she left behind. There was muffled chattering as Jenny led Rebecca through the door, and up the stairs. Daddy and Trip were invited indoors for a little conversation with chilled tea. There were so many questions. Nothing was sure anymore.

Jenny didn't really speak much. "Missus Becca, do you want your things with your other stuff?"

She looked around the room. Someone had set out a vase of glorious flowers. There was a lovely rag rug, fresh bed linens, a mirror, a tall armoire for hanging things, and a washstand with pitcher. Was this for one person? This was another world away from Franklin County hill country. Where was Trip? Where was Daddy? Why couldn't she hear what they said? Were they deciding things?

This was a dream. She walked over to where things were placed in the compartments of the armoire and touched each item that was already tucked inside. "Thank you, Jenny. When will I see my husband?"

"They had things to discuss, but I'm sure he will be up soon. Let me know when you need me." Then she left Rebecca to her thoughts.

Second Installment

Mama talked about those first years with Daddy like they were the glory days. All they had was each other. They were a team. They went deeper into the green Virginia hills. The first cabin wasn't much at all; but when the family was going to get bigger, neighbors and church people came over to build a more proper house and then an outbuilding. The land was good to them. They made it through the lean months with what had been stored up. People could be independent but could also rely on good friends. Rebecca thought being grown and married would be the best life of all. Don't know what she thought being the wife of John R. Spencer III would be like. She had just met all the people who already lived in the big house, her new home with new family. More than half the folks here were dark and liked to stay in the shadows. Slavery was the engine that powered the amazing industry that grew crops and raised livestock.

Her new husband, her daddy, and Old Sir John were somewhere having a conversation that was going to decide her future. Did she have no say? She had a lot that she could say, but they didn't want to hear any of it. The men held the reins because it didn't occur to them to do anything else. She should know they would give her what they thought would make her life good. "But how could they know what her heart told her about life? What was being agreed on in another part of the house where she was not included?"

She was left to sit. In the lovely new room that didn't know it belonged to her, she just sat. Until there was a knock at the door and the familiar voice of Trip who loved her dearly. That she knew with certainty. She knew that he would be her champion if only he could.

"Rebecca, it's your husband. Are you settled? Can I come in? How are you doing?"

His head poked in first, then he wrapped her in his arms. She was so grateful to see him.

"How would you like to go see Ginger? I can get you down to the stables to see your horse before you let Jenny help you get ready for supper. Everyone is anxious to know you. You will love them!"

"Where is Daddy?" She looked up with sad eyes.

"He's headed for home now, but Sir has agreed that you can go back to visit your mama and the kids when the weather is good, once a year. Everyone understands that you will miss them. You will get so you miss this place when you are away."

She wasn't going to worry about that right now. "Ginger is missing me now. Can we go to her?"

Down a back set of steps, they caught a glimpse of women and girls busy with pots, dishes, and piles of vegetables. They quickly turned to a porch and went out the back, side door. Every way she turned was a new shock. Nothing was like what she had known. When they made it to Ginger's stall, the girl and the horse stood silently, forehead to forehead for several minutes. The horse smelled like home. She breathed deep of the comfort it gave her. She wrapped her arms around the mare's smooth neck while Trip looked on. "Father understands that this horse is yours. You can go out for a ride whenever you want. Just tell the boys. The other mare was a gift from your family to ours," said the new husband, almost envious of the affection poured onto her loyal animal.

When they got back up to the house, Rebecca saw that Jenny had been waiting in the hall. She realized that Jenny had been given her care and education as a special task. Accustomed to being the one who took care of others, this was another startling development.

"Well Jenny, how did you get to have me as your job?" Rebecca was curious.

"I guess they know I can show you what is expected for the lady of the house. Plus, Mima is my mammy. She delivers all the babies, and we can take care of you." This told the new wife what she was supposed to do – make babies and be a lady. What a job description.

The two picked out a dress to wear for supper while Jenny described how the family took the evening meal together. And no, Rebecca would not be helping in the kitchen or with the serving. Getting into the new clothes was complicated enough. What a strange place. Her old life was over.

And that supper was another thing. People watched her every move. She was never sure what she did wrong when the children started to snicker. Trip tried to gently lead without appearing to correct her. Jenny watched anxiously from the edge of the room, making mental notes about what she should show to the new missus. If Rebecca continued to be the object of sport, any slave whose job was to help her learn, would be blamed. That was likely going to happen often enough.

Later Trip was confronted by his stepmother. "What did you expect? She's not one of us. She came from the hills. She'll never be able to be a true Spencer."

"You don't know her. She's better than anybody around her. She knows how to manage better than anybody I know. She is honest and loyal. When she's the mistress, you will see." This was not a comfort to Old Sir John's current wife. She was watching the future for own son crumble before her eyes."

From the first Rebecca was an easy target because she had stolen the heart of the future head of the plantation. Jealousy fanned the flames of all those addicted to drama who believed that telling the truth was optional. There were too many questions about what to believe. She could only rely on the children who were starved for attention. Sometimes though they mixed imagination with insight. Slaves in the house were careful about picking sides. They did not know how the power struggle and intrigue might affect their own lives. It was best to be neutral.

The main person to watch carefully was Old Sir John's current wife. She had something the family wanted for a long time, a little boy who could carry the Spencer name into the future. Trip was their first, then they had a long run of little girls. If Rebecca also had only girls too, Delila's baby James would eventually be head of the family. Delila would have a secure future, running the house as she saw fit. Rebecca was stepping on her future. The girl from the hills didn't understand what she could be stealing from this ambitious mother-in-law.

Some of the other women looked for ways to make her as miserable as possible. Where could they find her weaknesses? Hinting that Trip had other sweethearts was a favorite strategy. Making her insecure was too delicious. She was smart but not educated. How could they make her feel stupid? She was brave, so at any turn they would challenge her courage. If they could make her do something dangerous and get hurt, so much the better. The fruit that looked so shiny and perfect from the outside had a rotten middle.

When Rebecca became pregnant with her first child, Delila made a summer trip to Philadelphia to interview a new tutor for the children and do some shopping. There were potentially two little boys who would need proper training to become Virginia gentlemen. One of the shopping finds was a pair of gold earrings that would set off any face at formal events. Made using gold coins from before the revolution, this stunning jewelry would only work for a lady brave enough to pierce her ears. That would hurt and meant risking an infection after the work was done. Dangerous when the weather was hot. It looked like an innocent and generous gift.

Delila knew what the possibilities were when she presented them to the young mother-to-be. She sweetened the deal by saying Trip wanted Rebecca to have the pricey jewelry. Poor John was too embarrassed to say he really was not pushing for the piercing when Rebecca was expecting a child. But Delila made the case that this was a way to prove the depth of love Rebecca had for her husband.

The rest of the house waited to see what the decision would be. Earrings as fine as these would be worthy of passing down through generations, but they could exact a cost before the first child was even in the father's arms. This was a challenge, a test. Would it be accepted? Rebecca stepped into the power struggle and with her servant Jenny's help she weathered the primitive ear piercing. She became the owner of the expensive gift. Delila had expected to win either way. Being out maneuvered didn't please her. Rebecca was learning what to expect from people who were playing a cruel game and keeping score.

Running down the stairs and out to the stable, she was out to see her best friend. The gentle mare was aging, but Rebecca took her out for exercise every chance she had. The men had decided that she should always have a man ride along because they doubted that Ginger could outrun a cougar or bobcat lurking in the woods.

While the chaperone was looking for wild game, the girl took advantage of solitude to pour her heart out to the understanding horse.

"Ginger, you are the only one who understands that this place is not what Daddy thought it would be. You and I both are cared for in a way, but we have to pay for every kindness. The only thing I've done wrong is that I came from the hills. I can never be one of them. But I don't see them good to each other either. They push and shove to give each other fits. That's all they know. Mama knew, but I thought I knew better. If it could be just Trip with me, that would be different."

The big brown eyes of the horse were filled with love. She lived for moments of peace in the fresh air, away from people. Then the sound of a musket, hopefully bringing down supper across the hill, interrupted the healing moment. Her reflex was to get over the rise to see if she could be any help with what the man found in the woods. She would never get past the way she was raised. Now she was supposed to sit back and let others wait on her. How could she be so bad just the way she was?

Third Installment

There were sweet moments that made Rebecca wish all the more that things turned out differently. Jenny and her mother Mima took their work, birthing babies, seriously. They were an expert team of midwives, and Rebecca would have been an excellent mother if they hadn't whisked the baby away into the arms of the nanny at the very start. Rebecca was allowed to rock the baby and take care of minimal needs. Little Abe loved to hear his mother sing and would settle right down to be rocked with a lullaby. That was a joy.

Trip heard the words of a favorite song as he stood outside the door. That voice, that had charmed him when he was visitor to the Akers farm, still could wrap him in her spell. His love was only stronger with a brand-new son in the house.

> Hush, little baby, don't say a word,
> Mama's going to buy you a mockingbird.
> And if that mockingbird don't sing,
> Mama's going to buy you a diamond ring.
> And if that diamond ring turns brass,
> Mama's going to buy you a looking glass.
> And if that looking glass gets broke,
> Mama's going to buy you a Billy goat.
> And if that Billy goat won't pull,
> Mama's going to buy you a cart and bull.
> And if that cart and bull turn over,
> Mama's going to buy you a dog named Rover.
> And if that dog named Rover won't bark,
> Mama's going to buy you a horse and cart.
> And if that horse and cart fall down,
> You'll still be the sweetest little baby in town.

Baby and mother snuggled in, and she passed along the wisdom that her teenage heart wanted to share. "My sweet, sweet little one, all those things that we can buy may not make you happy. I just hope you can be as wonderful as your own handsome daddy."

He took that as his cue to make an entrance and join the loving scene. "You are a lovely mother with a precious baby son. I am the luckiest man alive! Someday we will be master and mistress and the people who live here will feel blessed."

But she had her own private thoughts. If only it had been just us making a life together with lovely little babies. I haven't been given the chance to be a proper mother.

Life on the plantation meant she was judged every day. Their looks of disapproval were used to keep her in line. They were working to make her into a proper southern lady. It was hard on everybody. If she did too well, that just seemed to make them mad. Outshining the women who were her betters was not a good idea. She spent hours on needle work and other solitary tasks. Some of the easiest people to talk to were the house staff who were expected to make everything run smoothly while staying in "their place."

Her refuge was out in the stables, not a ladylike place to be. The gentle Ginger who came with her on the wedding day was always waiting, aging there among the racing horses and the work horses. She watched as the men who managed the valuable beasts went about the day-to-day work. This was a place that felt most like the home place where she grew up. Occasionally it was acceptable to strike up conversation with people passing through, but she was definitely not part of the general plantation's commerce.

She hadn't been able to make the promised trip back to the Akers homestead. She needed to see Mama, Daddy, and the kids but when the time came, she was pregnant with Abraham. Old Sir John decided that it would be too risky to make the trip into the hill country. Sir John was thoughtful and gentle some of the time but could be stormy and demanding the rest of the time. It was like he thought only hard men who thundered around would be respected. Rebecca's mama said men like this were big babies throwing a fit when they didn't get their way.

Rebecca's own husband was more like her papa. He had a strength that her in-laws didn't see. Trip was so attentive and loving that after Abraham was born, in just a few months she was pregnant again. She kept it a secret as long as she could and started bringing up the promised reunion.

Trip was kept busy with responsibilities assigned to him by his father, but the decision was made to assign a driver and wagon to bring the little mother, a nurse, and baby to her parents' home. It was so exciting to load the bounty from produce on the plantation, a jug of honey, and some fresh baked goods from the kitchen under the cover of the wagon. She had been gathering little gifts for the children back at home to tuck into the load. Mama was going to get an embroidered apron and set of tea towels. Old Sir John also sent along a buyer to check on any of Daddy's horses that might be for sale. Now that they were kin, maybe the wagon can bring back fresh vegetables and some of the home brew rye whiskey.

Their traveling started before light in the morning, before the household had started to stir. The plan was to arrive by late morning. As they came closer to Rebecca's home, happy anticipation wrapped around the wagon's passengers. The baby in her arms was alert. She was sure the baby she was carrying in her tummy could feel the change too. The shade was cool and the lane familiar. This was great.

She thought she would burst when Mama stepped out on the porch. Rebecca leaped from the wagon and ran to the open arms and the explosion of brothers and sisters. Everybody wanted to see the baby. Abraham was theirs too. The driver and the trader tethered the horse and sat under a tree away from the family.

Rebecca looked around at the kids, greeting each with a hug, but noticing the growing legs and arms. She remembered them much smaller, and they seemed a little shy of her. In fairness, she had changed too. She was now a married lady with a new family and a new plan for her future, a future very different from what any of them could expect. The Spencer women had been relentless in their attempts to improve her while putting her in her place.

Especially different was her sister Adaline who was now Mama's chief lieutenant. She seemed to be proficient in all the skills necessary to run a home. Even though it was good to see Mama getting help with the heavy work of the house and children, Rebecca felt homesick for what would have been her place now filled by her sister. This visit that should have been nothing but happy was not what she'd expected. Had she expected everything to freeze in time while she was gone? She had been homesick, but homesick for the way it used to be.

Then she heard the shout that Daddy was coming back from the horse pen. Her strong and wonderful Daddy was coming up to the house. Daddy, the man who could charm a critter's wildness away. He understood their hearts, and they responded. He who commanded respect because of the deep respect he had for all God's creatures. Her hero was coming, and when she stepped out, she saw him approach, moving with a slight limp that had been added to his gait.

"I need to see that baby boy! Rebecca, you are a mama! I knew you would make a good match." After his welcome and the hug for his daughter, he held out his hands to hold the little one who made so many people happy. The baby's last name was Spencer, but he was part of the Akers clan too. The family circle was growing.

The family moved to benches under a shade tree with all the children gathered around. There was news to share. Rebecca needed to be told who had died and which neighbors packed up to move west. She was told who was now married and what was happening down at the trading post. There had been a lot of change in almost two years. Rebecca told them Ginger was older and better off waiting back at the plantation. She watched the confidence that had grown in Adaline in partnership with Mama. The women here were capable and loving, providing the energy to care for the needs of the household. They didn't sit back and order others around. She envied them their strength and ability.

Baby Abe had been basking in the smiling faces of all the little children who competed for his attention. His delight was obvious, until he completely wore out and needed to be held quietly in the nurse's arms. Rebecca saw the concern on her mama's face as the new baby was passed to a non-family member. She decided it was time to show them what she brought.

Everyone gathered around as they emptied the back of the wagon. The produce was appreciated, as was the honey and the amazing fresh baked bread. Mama started to frown as each little girl unwrapped a small clay pitcher with a painted face, just the right size for walnut shell teacups. Grandpa Fiddle Sticks, who mostly sat and rocked but was really there to help the girls in the kitchen at the Spencer place, had whittled a miniature horse for each of the boys.

Mama wasn't smiling. "This is really all too much. You are spoiling the kids." She had never had an apron and towel set quite so nice.

"Please, Mama" Rebecca pleaded. "I wanted to do this. You are all still kin."

While all the others put together the afternoon's dinner, Daddy wandered off with the trader to look at the stock pen to talk horses. There were a couple that Old Sir John would be interested in, and they arranged a price. They also loaded the wagon with vegetables and some jugs of rye.

After filling up on home cooking and stories, Rebecca prepared herself for the ride back to Trip. Daddy said to tell Sir John many thanks for letting her come.

Then Mama took her aside and said, "All my children are special and will deal with life in their own way, but you always have been different. Think about how you chose Trip and made up your own mind about the wedding. You consider things, and you're smarter than most. Then you act. That won't necessarily make life easy on you, but you are a survivor. I wish I could live long enough to see all that will become of you." Then she added, "Careful not to change too much, Becca. Your people are here, not in some fancy house."

Riding back to the Spencer place gave her time to think about how her life had been changing. One was sure, nothing ever seemed to stay the same. Where was the place that she was meant to be? Can't go back, that was the only certain thing.

Fourth Installment

On the ride back home, the baby slept, and they traveled in silence. Rebecca had time to think. Who was she now? Who was she meant to be? She had married the first-born son of Sir John R. Spencer II. His papa intended him to be the one to carry the legacy, to continue to build the wealth that would be the envy of the family that had been left behind across the ocean, English nobility. A new country was growing, and the colony of Virginia was the obvious place where the intelligent, educated leadership would be found. This was a new world, and the Spencer family-owned land grew massive fields of cash crops, filled stables with magnificent horses, and ran it all with livestock and over 100 slaves.

The women were pampered and lived in luxury. They were entitled to life resembling the upper class in the countries of Europe. There was the problem. Her future seemed determined by a society of ladies. Ladies who treated her like an outsider who hadn't earned the right to marry old Sir John's son. She could do nothing to suit them. And she wasn't sure how hard she wanted to try anymore.

Her husband was the only one who had actually seen her strength and understood her nature. Rebecca's first born was a son, which pleased everyone, at least those who counted. The little one she carried in her tummy had started to move with the same vigor as Abraham. That might be a boy too. She seemed to be the one who had successful pregnancies. Were the other women too delicate? Could she be the one to have the promise of more male heirs to fill the house? There were a lot of little girls already who would need to find husbands somewhere else. Her mother-in-law was not pleased. She had just one little boy who now came after Rebecca's husband in succession, followed by Abraham, who was to be groomed for a future role.

When she first met Trip, she didn't understand that he went by a nickname. He was John R. Spencer III. He was different from the others who came to her daddy to trade livestock and buy produce. He fell in love with her and the joy that filled her home. She didn't know that households with so much wealth could be so full of ambition and suspicion. The Spencer family found very little joy in the imposing walls and cushioned chairs.

She arrived back at the plantation late and was met by Old Sir John and Trip. "It's good to be home. Little Abraham was good as gold, and everybody loved him. We had no trouble at all. You should see what they sent you."

Trip helped his wife and son down from the wagon. They went up to the room with the nurse right behind carrying the baby's things. The driver and the trader circled the bed of the wagon to show Old Sir John the generosity of Rebecca's family back in the hill country.

The next day was strange. Everything was the same, but somehow, she was different. She had questions about her future. What did her father-in-law and his current wife feel should be her future? Did that match the person she could see herself becoming? Could it be the pregnancy was giving her moods? Why did she feel this way?

Rebecca's house servant, Jenny, made sure she was ready for her day. She was now also a nanny for baby Abraham. Casual chatter was natural as the two women greeted each other.

"How was your travel? Did you have a good visit with your family?"

"We had a good visit I suppose, but it wasn't like I thought it would be."

"How is that?"

"They've changed. I should have expected the kids to grow. My sister Adaline is now working with Mama to run the house. That was supposed to be my job, but I wasn't there anymore. There isn't really a place for me anymore. And both Mama and Daddy are older."

"Guess when you are not there, things move along?"

"But I thought I was the same. Now I've got to thinking. I've probably changed too. I'm not hill country anymore." Rebecca looked slowly around the room.

"No ma'am, you are here." Jenny sympathized.

"That's just it, Jenny. I don't know if I'm part of here either. A lot of the folks are always wanting to get ahead of each other. They can't stand to be the one behind! Like being second or third in line is a sin greater than anything." She turned to the one person she dared to share her mind with. "Jenny, I don't think I'm even in their same kind of line. I'm different from all those others."

"I don't think you're so wrong, ma'am."

As the days passed Rebecca thought about her situation. She kept on telling Trip how much she enjoyed getting back to her home place. She knew the way, she could handle her own hunting rifle, and she wouldn't need as much of an escort. Little Abraham loved the cool mountain air. But the other thing was soon obvious to everyone. Another baby was on the way. The decision makers on the plantation didn't want her to make any visit until the next Spencer child was born.

Rebecca was spending more time with Abraham, taking him with her out to see the horse that carried his mother to the Spencer place. He learned respect for all the animals out in the stock yard. There were those who worked with powerful strength to sustain life on the plantation. There were those who were pampered and beautiful, bred to win bragging rights at the racetrack. He understood that the stallions, standing tall in separate sections, were often ill-tempered and wanted to command the herd of mares. This was their nature. The strongest would breed to produce the most impressive foals.

It occurred to her that perhaps her willfulness and comfort with the animals may have been part of why Old Sir John saw her as a good match for his more sweet-natured son. He was clearly interested in seeing a strong line of men from the union of Trip and Rebecca. Some of the very qualities that made her have the approval of father-in-law, were the qualities that were so aggravating to her mother-in-law. How could such an unladylike person have approval from Sir Spencer? Delila's own son, James, lost position on the plantation every time Trip and Rebecca had a baby boy. She wanted to make Rebecca pay for that! Delila was clearly jealous.

Rebecca's new baby was probably going to be even bigger than Abe, and Abraham was tall for his age compared to the other children. Lucky for the expectant mom that Jenny and her mother knew just what to do for the health of all. Birthing had a way of bringing the women even closer together. Isaac greeted the world with gusto. There were days when she brought both boys out to give them rides on Ginger's back like she did for the children at home with Daddy and Mama. Sometimes she brought one of Jenny's kids along, if it was OK with Sir John. Isaac was progressing even faster than his brother had.

Seeing the kids, black and white, playing together soothed her mind. Jenny was supposed to be less able than the white folks, but she understood what it meant to be a mother and was a model that Rebecca envied. Jenny settled "territory disputes" that were part of play for children with gentleness and love. She knelt down, eye-level with potential combatants, and discussed how they would like to resolve the dispute and still be friends. Rebecca wanted to be a parent like Jenny, with calm fairness. As a nanny, Jenny knew what each child was thinking and had a storehouse of distractions that would bring everyone together.

The "gentle" ladies on the plantation didn't tolerate childish behavior. When noise reached a level of discomfort, children were hustled off to the care of another. Or justice was delivered with the back of a hand. The reaction was random and seemed to be more connected to adult's level of frustration.

It didn't take any time at all for Trip and Rebecca to be expecting a third child. Now there was urgency again to visit family in the hill country before Rebecca's condition became more obvious. It would be so good to be back with the Akers kin with her two little boys. Then a traveler from the south stopped by the plantation with heart-breaking news.

The neighbor came to let Rebecca know that her daddy had an accident while clearing a fallen tree off the trail. His limp had been getting worse, and he didn't move as fast. Things shifted, and he was pinned under a fallen limb. He was gone quickly. The preacher was called, and they had a proper funeral, a comfort to the widow Akers. The eldest daughter, Adaline married Aaron last spring, and her husband was now running the place. It was sure hard to lose Daddy and think about another in his place.

Rebecca's heart had dreamed that Daddy was going to live forever. He had been her rock. Mama must be shattered. Maybe she would find comfort seeing Abraham and Isaac, Daddy's image in miniature. She redoubled her efforts to organize the wagon ride to the home place.

Whether it was out of sympathy or because the distraught daughter-in-law was so persuasive, Old Sir John agreed to the trip just the way she proposed it. She could manage the boys and drive the team, keeping her hunting rifle handy in case of problems. Just one trader would be required to go with them. That man would guard the wagon's passengers and negotiate for new stock if they were ready for sale of animals.

Out of respect for the fact that her mama was now a widow, Rebecca was able to pack up a generous supply of food prepared by the kitchen along with produce from the plantation gardens. They packed extra sets of clothes for all the children. Her own boys picked out special toys they thought the kids would like. The trader was given a pouch of coin and a bundle of tobacco to sweeten the deal if a purchase should be made.

It took only a couple days to prepare. The weather was favorable and traveling went well. The home place was a welcome site, but roof, steps, and front porch now made a sad face in her imagination. A reunion with family members should have been more comforting than it was, but there was a shift. Daddy's place was now filled by a stranger. Mama looked fragile. She sagged just like the house. Rebecca was thanked for the wagon full of gifts, but there was an edge. She suspected them of accusing her of showing off the abundance of the wealthy plantation. Nobody said it, but she could feel it. She wasn't one of them anymore. She actually made an excuse to go back earlier than planned.

Mama stood by the team of horses to wish safe travels, then moved in close and said, "They want you to be like them, daughter. But I don't think you can. I can see you moving away from us too. Life only goes forward." And with a long, sad hug she said her goodbye.

Fifth Installment

As they approached the Spencer land, Rebecca considered the changes Adaline's new husband, Aaron, was making now that Daddy passed. She always felt Daddy's touch was magic. Buyers came from a distance because the care he put into everything made for superior livestock. It would never have occurred to him to be a brute to have command. He worked with trust and respect. He firmly disagreed with buying slaves to help with the farm, though sometimes he had a hired man. Aaron thought Daddy was a fool. He talked about making the property produce more income. The cheapest way was to buy a few slaves. Sure, he would have to feed and clothe them, but in the long run he would come out ahead. It was business.

Rebecca was uneasy with the whole idea. In a lot of little ways, she was surprised by how people didn't think. Old Sir John considered himself a fair-minded man who treated people well, but he didn't think of everything. When the servants cleaned the dining room floor, making the wood shine, the Spencer men would walk thought the house leaving clumps of mud for the work to be done again. Cleaning on the floor was what she did at home, and now she was told that this work was only for inferior people who were not so smart. People believed their slaves didn't have the same sensibilities as their "betters".

The overseers in the field were expected to use the harshest methods to get every worker to put in a full day. When the wind was right, she heard everything happening in the yard. She would flinch with each blow. When she and Trip were Master and Mistress, could she convince her husband to change this treatment. Was she asking too much?

How could her servant Jenny be inferior when Rebecca learned so much from her? It was right in front of her eyes, and she was taught to believe what she saw. It seemed that when you were raised trusting the slave system, there was no way to admit what was plain as day. When faced with the obvious lie, people worked just that much harder to find ways to justify staying the same.

She was not expecting the conversation she would be having with Old Sir John when she returned. But it was coming.

Rebecca and the boys stayed overnight and returned late the next afternoon, but it was not the same warm welcome that she had after the first visit. Her husband joined his returning family, but he said father wanted to talk to her in the morning. Did Sir John think that her visit would not be done in just one day? What went wrong. The next day she found out.

"Rebecca, I've been generous with you, and you make my son very happy. For that I am grateful. But I am disappointed that you did not tell me everything about this visit."

She listened quietly. "What do you mean?"

"Family is very important to me; I think you know that. Now I heard from my wife that she thinks you were taking risks with my grandchildren."

What has that witch said to him? Delila hates me and would say anything. Rebecca wondered what would come next.

"She has heard that you went back into the hill country knowing full well that you and Trip are expecting another son. Don't you know that in your condition you should be very careful about unnecessary travel." He was as cross as he had ever been with her. "I want to know that I can trust you."

"I wasn't sure about a baby, and I am feeling healthy. I am strong and have no problem with babies." She had guessed she was pregnant but needed to get back to see Mama after Daddy died. Didn't he see that. There is no way to know for sure about pregnancies until the baby starts to move.

"And this isn't the first time. You did the same thing the first time, before Isaac. I chose to ignore it because I had promised your Daddy you could have visits. I am a man of my word. But I can't have this carelessness."

"I am so sorry," she began. "I was very grateful to have the time with my family. I am sure that my time with them only makes a baby stronger. It won't happen again."

"No, it won't. We'll see to that." He ended with a stare that seemed to dare her to protest.

"Yes, Sir." With that she left looking at the floor. This could have been much worse. She needed to get away and went directly up to her quarters. She knew she would be fine on a wagon. Women always did that, but she also knew she was being deceptive when she didn't tell about the new baby she could be carrying for the Spencer household.

When she found Jenny with the boys, she breathed deep and broke into a silent smile seeing her two precious darlings. All attention was on Isaac, teaching him to call Jenny "Mammy," Rebecca was the "Mama". Jenny was so natural with children. She was also born to be a healer. It was a blessing to have her right there to help with recovering after births. A blessing in many ways, because these children were coming quickly.

"Jenny, you are the light of my days. Don't know what I'd do without you." She burst out this praise for the woman she trusted with everything important.

Just then Trip came striding into the room. "Hey, what about me!" He smiled as he wrapped his arms around his wife. "I hope you are alright after that visit with Sir."

"Oh, I'm fine. I probably should have let everyone know that there could be another baby coming. But I was fine. I needed to see Mama." Rebecca made her confession and made excuse all at once. Being truthful was part of her nature. This was cleansing.

"He just is very protective of his family. Our children are one of his concerns. And this was the second time you made a visit that he thought was dangerous." Trip was hoping that she understood why this was so important to the Spencer Plantation.

Rebecca turned to look him in the eye and said, "Trip, have you ever thought about setting up our own place. Working it just the two of us and making out own decisions, earning our own way. We could do it. We could be happy."

"And I would have you all to myself? You make it sound like a dream, but how would we manage. All my life I've been told that I have responsibility for this land and all these people. I am what they are expecting keep them clothed and fed, to carry the family name."

"We could do it," she replied. "Mama and Daddy raised all us kids to know how to care for ourselves. I am young and strong. What I don't know, I can learn. I can make you happy in a place where we are free to make our own life. Let someone else run this farm."

"Oh Rebecca, the farm and I are a package deal. You are tired and stressed and still grieving for your Daddy. Give yourself time. It's good here. Whenever you need something, anything, just let me know. I will make sure people know how good and sweet and smart and wonderful you are."

She relaxed in his arms. She wanted to stay with this man forever. In that moment it didn't matter that there were people who couldn't stand her very presence on Spencer land.

He continued to soothe her as she listened. "I want you to know this with certainty. Your welfare means more to me than anything else. Anything. I am happy when you stay strong and happy. You are the one I chose for life."

"You are my angel," she replied.

And a new baby did arrive a few months later. Samuel became part of her gang of boys. She was surprised how much she enjoyed the rough and tumble brothers trailing behind her out to the stables, baby on her hip. She made sure that they understood how to follow her instruction, to respect the animals and even be part of their care. Rebecca wanted them to have the same comfort with powerful animals that she felt. But she also wanted them to have wariness that would help them expect the unexpected. There were a few with ugly tempers that they should avoid. She wanted them to survive.

She was not the only one who noticed how strong and bright her boys were becoming. The father and grandfather were proud. Her children had excellent manners, but also the spine to stand up when challenged. The loyalty of siblings was undeniable, as well as the competition between brothers. Abraham was soon old enough for his lessons with the tutor. The school master said he was very quick.

Rebecca knew better than to ask to make another visit with family back home. She could tell that there would be a fourth baby. She quietly stayed on the plantation, but she would have loved to take the boys to see the place where she grew up. They should know about the shady hills and streams that were even more beautiful than fertile farmland.

Then the unthinkable happened. The flu went through the Spencer Plantation in the winter before the baby was to be born. One after another, people took to their sick beds. It was roughest out in the slave quarters where many people died. It didn't spare the big house either. Many people felt the effects of the illness long after the original infection had moved on. Trip, for some reason, carried a cough that never let up. There was no reason why other people were spared and never seemed to suffer at all. Some were left weak for a month.

After everyone felt the worst was over, Trip went out to work with the field and returned with a fever. A crushing cough began to strangle his breath. Sir John, Rebecca, and a few of the others stayed by him as much as they could. Then Rebecca was ushered away thinking to protect her unborn baby. Trip's magnificent heart quit beating just two months before his fourth child was born. When his heart stopped, other hearts were broken.

This last child was born a little early, but with the same gusto as her brothers. People saw her delicate, feminine features but felt the impact of her forceful personality. She was busy every minute exploring the world. A lot of folks commented on how they saw her mother in her, not always in an approving way.

There were other changes too. The mood in the plantation was beginning to change. With Trip gone, long nourished jealousies began to shine through. Delila once again started promoting the interests of her own son, James. Children with other mothers started to look for weaknesses in Abraham, Isaac, and Samuel. Nothing needed to be directed at Rebecca herself, but adults started to dismiss, as normal childish behavior, episodes that should have been corrected. Everyone knew she could not ignore this. Rebecca's instincts were alerted to harm that may come to her children.

Could she be everywhere at once? Could she really protect them? Where was the powerful father who would spread his arms around them? How bad could this get?

Sixth Installment

Rebecca looked for a way to deal with other children who were starting to pick at her boys. Before her husband passed it was a given that she and Trip would one day be the authority, the decision maker. Their children should have been favored, nobody should have challenged their "king of the hill" status. But now Trip died and left his father still running the place. She had never had to deal with Abraham, Isaac, or Samuel being a target for other children. If she went to Old Sir John to see what he would recommend, his advice would have been as expected. Anyone who defied him should expect to be sorry they even tried. He would have enforced consequences for any slight or infraction. She knew that an offender's response would be resentment and defiance. There had to be a better way to make her sons respected and able meet a challenge with strength. She had to do something.

She started by inviting other kids to join in the rides with the ever-patient Ginger. This horse had worked with children from the moment she became a birthday present to Rebecca. When children asked why Ginger was with the horses who would race and not the work horses, she explained that Ginger was past the day of heavy work. Her poor old body was not up to it. She was still good for rides. She was a special horse who kept Abraham's mother company when she moved from the farm where she grew up.

She was Rebecca's partner as she taught everyone how to work as friends. This was an investment of time that was intended to pay off, helping her boys to have allies. Like what her daddy said, "The best way to get rid of enemies was to turn them into friends." Her babies were growing into boys. She wanted her boys to be seen as leaders for a group.

The new country was growing like children. More and more travelers stopped and enjoyed the hospitality of John Spencer. There were people heading west to the territories. Some were coming back east for business in places like Philadelphia or the Federal District. Some just stopped for water; others had lively conversation over supper.

She sat and listened when the conversation turned to the land available to the west, and how settlers who worked hard could make a life for themselves. It was a fresh start for many people. It sounded like the dream she had while her husband was alive. She couldn't go back to where she grew up, and she certainly didn't fit in with the Spencer family. Wasn't there some place she belonged?

The politics of the day were hotly debated. The new President was married to a lady who wasn't yet divorced. His marriage wasn't legal. Next came the "Petticoat Affair." This President was pushing for tariff on imports coming in from Europe, affecting big plantations like the Spencer's. He said the national bank caused problems with the economy and wanted to do away with it. He was cleaning out all the "corrupt" officials from the earlier administration, replacing them with his own. Rebecca sometimes dared to make a comment or two when she couldn't contain herself. The other women were embarrassed by her nerve. The gentlemen smiled when they saw how uncomfortable Old Sir John became. She never seemed to learn.

One hot afternoon, doing needle work on the porch, she was tearing out stitch after stitch. There were voices going out to the stables. Soon there was an agitated commotion in the horse barn. She put her sewing aside and hurried in that direction, but the unbelievable was already happening. The horses left in the barn were calling out and hitting into the railings on the stalls. Her heart sank to her stomach as she found that cries for help were coming from her dear friend Ginger. Two field hands had her hitched to a fully loaded wagon that was miring in the mud. She had buckled to her knees. The stripes on her flanks showed marks of the whip.

"What are you doing?" she demanded, even though it was obvious they were breaking the gentle horse's heart.

"We were told this animal should earn its keep," came the reply. "The Missus says she is a nag and needs to pay her way."

She saw the light dimming from Ginger's eyes as the agony of betrayal brought her down. Old John's wife had gone too far. Rebecca quit thinking and moved with blind purpose toward where the other horses were kept. She opened the gate to the exercise yard with precision and cleared the way for the two prize stallions to enter and end the violent rivalry that drove them mad for months. People in the yard could not believe what they were seeing. The power in the carnage was a fight to the death. No mere human could stop this. They stood in shock. It happened so rapidly.

Rebecca sank to the ground in a flood of tears, rocking back and forth. What had she done? What had she done?

Someone carried her to her room and put her to bed. She slept for a long, long time. There was no redeeming what she had done. She could not forgive herself. The whispers around the house told the story of Rebecca going crazy.

Mama's parting words rumbled through her mind. "They want you to be like them, daughter. But I don't think you can. Life only goes forward." The empty words of comfort Trip used while he was still alive were hollow, "I want you to know this with certainty. Your welfare means more to me than anything else. Anything. I am happy when you stay strong and happy. You are the one I chose for life." Now was this hopeless?

The rest of the plantation followed its daily routine and gave her enough space so they would not be infected by her lack of reason. She thought about her future, if there was to be a future for her.

Coming up the lane to the big house rode a stranger from the west. He was traveling light, all by himself, and tied up at the rail in front of the house. Beggars looking for a handout always went around to the back and looked for a kitchen. This man let his horse take water from the trough and looked over the people in the yard. There were groups of very little children with black nannies. A couple white boys made the approach as they left the thin woman who had to be their mama.

"Hey, mister," the tallest one spoke right up. "Do you need something?"

"Well, yes, I do. I have business with John Spencer. I'm here to look him up," said the stranger.

"That's my grandpa. I'm Abe. You can call me Abraham," replied the little boy. "What's your name?"

A warm smile spread across the visitor's face. "I'm Sam Turner. You can call me Mr. Turner. Where might Mr. Spencer be? I've been told that Sir John may be looking for an expert trader to hire on as an agent."

"I believe he's in the study today. I can make sure he knows you are here." What a formal reply for the little fellow.

"Is your friend here your brother?" Mr. Turner asked. When the boys both nodded, he put his hand in his saddle bag and said, "Since you have greeted me so nicely, I have something I picked up in the woods on the way over here. Would you each like a hickory nut?"

The woman had quietly advanced and said, "What are you fixing to give my boys? If it's something eat, my little one has a touchy tummy."

"Okay," he replied. "How about they each have just one. And if that doesn't cause problems you can give them two more." He held out more of the little nuts.

About that time Old Sir John appeared on the porch and invited him inside.

When someone new arrived with news to share, everyone on the farm was eager to hear. Mr. Turner had been recommended by a friend as being excellent at making deals. Both a buyer and a seller, he had the knack for reading people. He knew what was going through their minds and could manage top dollar for what he had to sell. Old Sir John liked the idea of having someone young to send out as a trustworthy representative after his oldest son, Trip, passed away.

As it worked, Turner was likeable. He seemed to enjoy the children who were brave enough to seek him out. He was funny and could charm everybody. Old Sir John was pleased with his ability to deliver as promised.

Turner taught people a new card game that soon became frowned upon as a time waster. In deference to Old Sir John, he didn't share any more from his storehouse of 'time wasting' pastimes. He thrived on risks. He loved taking chances, and he seldom lost a bet.

He became a favorite story-teller about all the wonders he saw while traveling in the west. He described wide rivers that were highways for all manner of boats and rafts and canoes. There was wild game and rich back soil. He'd made acquaintances with native nations and found them excellent trading partners. He had even been into a northern section of wilderness that was now the Wisconsin Territory, open for settlement. He spoke highly of the Sauk nation. They lived along the Des Moines River. It emptied into the great Mississippi. This green and abundant place called to Rebecca in her imagination.

But not everyone was happy. Sir John's current wife continued to distrust Rebecca's status as widow of the first son, John R. Spencer III. She found Rebecca's behavior a troubling challenge. When she took her husband aside, she listed all the daughter-in-law's irrational and willful behaviors. Wasn't it time to find this girl a new husband, a husband who would deal with a firm hand. She needed someone who could rein her into the proper submissive womanly role. If she had to leave all four children here on the Spencer Plantation, Jenny was a perfectly capable nanny who would raise them properly. They could still arrange visits.

Rebecca learned of this new plan for her future the same day as a messenger rode in from the south with the news the Mama passed away back on the Akers home place. Mama lost a lot of her strength after she lost Daddy. Adaline was now running the animals and the stills with her husband Aaron. She took care of the other siblings and had one on the way.

This was too much. Daddy, then Trip, then Ginger, and now Mama. Was she going to lose Abraham, Isaac, Samuel, and Sissy too? Was she going to lose herself with a husband selected because he could break her spirit? She had no one to turn to but herself, but what could she do? She turned to prayer and needed guidance, not just a table grace. There were no good choices, but there had to be a way to give her children a future and have one for herself as well. What did she really want in her future? How would she get there? It took a lot of tears before she faced it, but Mama had given her one last gift. She may have to take a chance and hope to be shown the way.

Seventh Installment

Rebecca wasn't good at lying. How could she face him and do this? She knew that Old Sir John was not a fool. He felt he had been good to her. But this house had cruelty, more than she could bear. They thought she was going mad, and maybe she was.

He heard her respectful knock at the door. "Yes, of course, I was actually expecting you. I was sorry to hear that your mother passed." So, he was expecting her and probably had an idea what she was about to ask.

"I am here today to ask about taking the children to pay our respects back home. I know it would be a comfort to everyone to see them." Rebecca looked at her feet, avoiding his eyes.

"This visit is important to you, I'm sure. But the children barely know their family. Maybe they could just stay here." His tone was consoling.

"Abraham, our oldest, and Isaac talk about them frequently. They visited after Daddy passed. People would love to see the baby and little Samuel. You promised my daddy that I would have trips back. Seems a child should know who their kin folks are." She looked up and saw him thinking. The bargaining was beginning. She had played her first card.

"Rebecca, you would have a hard time with four little ones in your wagon. Have you thought of that?" He was appealing to her reason, if she had any left.

"Yes, I suppose Jenny could come too, to help with the babies, of course." Would he agree to this? She had to try. Her skill as a midwife made Jenny a valuable slave to him.

"No, she might be needed here. Big Tom's girl is due any day with their third. She should stay here and take care of little Samuel and Sissy. Jenny has to stay close by. The big boys might like a ride into the hill country to see people they know." She had played the second card.

This loss couldn't stop her. She had to keep trying. "I will need to take presents for the kids. And something for Adaline's kitchen. My sister doesn't have the wonderful cooking things that we have here on the farm." She was hoping for a small win with this ask.

"Of course, and some bundles of tobacco. They would appreciate some of our corn and produce from the gardens. We can share." Old Sir John was being generous and also making a point about the wealth of the plantation to remind those hill people of their place.

"And some of the flour, sugar, and staples?" she asked.

"Of course. Whatever you want." His pride was making this part easy for her. She had played her next card.

Even though she couldn't take Jenny and the babies, she had to keep going. "This visit, I would like more time with aunts and uncles and cousins. It may be the last time we get to see them. How about this would be a week?" Would she win this card?

Sir John countered, "That may be a little long. You don't need any more than four days. You don't want to tire yourself out. This has been an exhausting time for you."

Now what? What was he thinking? "Oh, you are so right," she tried flattery. "You always know what is best." Four days is better than just one day. She had one more card to play.

"And I can handle the wagon on my own. You know that I'm as good a shot as any man. I can take care of problems." She had to make this one last request.

"I was thinking to send along a horse trader, if you don't mind. They would help you protect the children," he said. The chaperone had to be someone he could trust to make sure she didn't have an episode and do something to endanger the children.

"I really appreciate this. You are so good to me and the children." Rebecca wasn't getting everything she needed, but she couldn't lose her nerve now. She started to mentally list what valuables absolutely must go in the wagon like her jewelry, anything valuable that she might use for trading. She also had to decide how she must deal with the man sent to bargain for horses and keep an eye on her. She thanked Sir John.

Old Sir John sent for Mr. Turner. He had a mission for him. As the men sat and talked, Sir John described the job he had in mind for his agent. Turner was told to look for a male horse that could be kept for a breeding stallion back at the plantation. If the Akers only had a colt that had already been gelded, that would not work. Also find an older horse for Rebecca to help her with the loss of Ginger. She took comfort in that animal. There would be extra bundles of tobacco and money to seal the deal. The main thing for Turner, however, would be to keep an eye out to protect the boys. Abraham was John III's oldest, and he's smart enough to be in charge of the family one day. Rebecca might be unpredictable, and nothing bad should happen to the grandsons.

"Are you worried that something might happen?" asked Mr. Turner.

"I get an uneasy feeling from my daughter-in-law," Sir John answered. "People tell me she needs a firmer hand than I can give her. I really want the best for her, but I can see that she has problems taming her contrary nature. She isn't the best for the children." Turner's head began a slow nod as he considered the meaning behind the words he just heard.

"I see. I will make sure everything is just fine." As Turner left, he knew he should be careful.

Rebecca was having her own meeting. The stairs to the top floor had never felt so steep. She knew what she needed to do. Jenny, the ever-faithful nanny, would be rocking Sissy while watching Samuel play with little, whittled horses.

Rebecca sat on the edge of the bed so their eyes would be at the same level as she shared what she had to say. "Jenny, you have no idea how important you have been to me. I want you to remember that I know you love my children like they are your own. In many ways, they are yours as much as mine. I must make life difficult for people in this house. I can't help being who I am. Guess I can't change, but please don't believe everything they say about me."

"What I know, Missus Spencer, is that you love all these little ones and you treat me better than I ever dreamed you would." Jenny's frown meant that she didn't know what Rebecca was trying to tell her.

"Jenny, please… I'm counting on you." With a heavy breath, Rebecca turned to go down to the yard to help load the wagon. This needed to happen before she lost her nerve.

The travelers rolled away from the plantation before the sun was even close to rising. A nearly full moon kindly lit the way. They should be at the Akers place by midday. Abraham and Isaac were excited about the ride back into the hill country to see Mama's family. They only had snatches of memory from the last trip south. Even though there was a comfortable little "nest" with the supplies back in the bed, it took them a while to settle down and go to sleep. The night sounds and the wagon rocking back and forth eventually did the work of a comforting lullaby.

Rebecca had asked Mr. Turner to ride on the seat with her, but she kept the reins. She was signaling that she was in charge. Once the boys were lost in dreams she opened conversation with the farm's agent.

"Mr. Turner, this ride is not going to go like you've been told. Hope you are OK with that."

"That so?" He looked at her cautiously. The whole strange assignment was getting even stranger.

"I've thought about this, and I can't go back to the Spencer place. That farm is like poison to me. There's people there who have hated me from the time I arrived. They live to knock me down. Something inside me is dying. They have plans to get rid of me. I don't see a choice."

"You sure about that? Sir John wants to get a new horse for you while we're there. He wants you to be happy."

"He thinks God gave him the right to choose for everybody else. But I know what he's going to do, even if he doesn't. It's already in the works. They want to find me a new husband who will be quick to use the strap and the fist to make sure I know my place. They want to take away my children, all my children." She turned fierce. "I can't choose to go along with that while there's still any other way"

He was quiet, then said, "Your kids? How can they take the kids?" This ugly business was turning around in his mind.

"Those kids are theirs too, and they don't want me around. They want people to say I'm unfit," she said. "But don't worry. I've thought it through, and if you have any compassion for what will happen, and I think you might, we'll just part ways at the next fork. I'll head west and go around by the corn fields. You can go on straight. Do a little hunting or something before you go back. You can tell them that I had an accomplice who jumped you. When you came to, you had no idea where we went. You can keep Sir John's trading money to give back to him. He'll like that. You can convince them. I know you can. You can even take them back to try to hunt me down, but the boys and I will be long gone."

"Just where will you be going?"

"Somewhere out west. Don't know. Somewhere with room to start over. I can use the stuff in this wagon, hire a guide, and trade for what I need to start up a home place. I'll figure it out."

"And the boys? Who will protect them?"

"I will. I am their mother!"

"You will need a guide you can trust, who knows the land and a few folks, a guy who knows how to get things done."

"I will figure it out. There's no place for me in the hills with my sister, and I can't go back to John Spencer."

"Lady, I've never met any woman like you," he paused, took a breath, and paused again. "I can always get new work, but I can't always choose to do the right thing. I know the trails and the people. I'll get you to the territories."

Why was she being offered help? God must have sent an angel. "I can't turn that down. They say sometimes I am a problem. Promise you won't take it back."

"I promised Sir John I would make everything turn out fine. I just didn't say how I would do that." He wondered how she had convinced him, but he resolved to do it.

The right-hand turn was just ahead. They began the journey west.

Eighth Installment

For a while they rode briskly, but quietly, then Mr. Turner took control. "If I'm going to be the guide, I will have to take the lead, Mrs. Spencer," he said. "I know the trails, and I know how things work out here. You got this whole thing going, and I'm still not sure how. Now, we've got to do nothing that will make anybody back there suspicious that you went in a different direction. The longer they think that you are just visiting kin, the more of a head start we will have."

"I will follow your guidance, but you will have to listen to me when I have opinions," she responded, folding her arms.

He looked her straight in the eyes. "This is serious for you, but I'm pretty sure things would not go well for me if they were to head us off."

She softened a bit. "I understand that, and I greatly appreciate your assistance, Mr. Turner. When we get to a place where the boys and I can settle, I promise to split the first of whatever I can get growing. I am going to make this happen."

"You've not been treated right back there. I guess I was ready for a change, and helping with your predicament is a big change," he responded. "I think you deserve a chance to live your life with those kids. Never been part of something like that before."

"I was never cut out to sit still and be waited on, definitely not to own slaves. Never felt right. I wasn't born for that world." She had pain written on her face.

"For now, we want to get as far away from Spencer land as we can without making anybody think we are running. We don't want to be interesting to talk about. We need to be as ordinary as apple pie."

Rebecca looked at the two sleeping children and wondered if she really did know what she was doing. They would need to make the most of daylight but stop early enough to let the adults rest up. The road west had seen many families attempting passage out of the rugged mountains. Both Mr. Turner and Rebecca had to be alert to narrow trails with steep rock walls and treacherous drops to rivers rushing out toward the plains. Every time a little face looked over the side of the wagon into the ravine below, a cold finger ran up her spine. Was she risking their lives because she needed to get away?

As the next few days passed, they made good time but tried not to look like anybody was chasing them. When they stopped near a farmhouse to rest and let the children out to run about, they had a story to tell the farmer. It technically wasn't really a story. It was the truth, with a lot of truth left out. Rebecca was a widow. Turner had been hired by the lady's father-in-law to escort the little family to their relatives. Her husband's people thought she would be better off with them.

This made it easy to remember the "story" which actually wasn't a "story." It was only natural that the boys called him "Mr. Turner." No worry that the children would raise suspicion telling something that didn't match up with what they needed people to believe.

Rebecca did her best to make the ride into an adventure, distracting the children from the perilous drops. Abraham and Isaac were to keep track of any new or unusual animals and plants as they covered more ground. Their mom encouraged each boy to start a pretty rock collection to take with them in the wagon bed. She helped their fragile little fingers play Cat's Cradle or make a braid of long grass found growing beside still water. She had them sing along to church songs. They naturally enjoyed all the

Christmas carols, not caring about the season. She also made sure they knew the tune to "Amazing Grace" and "Thousand Tongues to Sing."

Mr. Turner called them his troops. When they stopped for the night, he made sure they gathered enough sticks and small branches for a little fire. They watched him start the evening's fire that would give them comfort as they bedded down. He assured them that wild animals didn't like the fire, and this would help keep them safe. They followed him around, and Rebecca could see how much having a man who was interested in them meant to boys. When she lost her husband, they lost a daddy. Turner had to be as travel weary as she was, but he stood straighter, and his face softened when they looked up to him.

For a while they ate from the food that had been packed for them back at the plantation. There were also lucky finds. A few edible wild things would fill their bellies. Mr. Turner said it would be good for him to hire on to do chores if people needed a hand. He could make wagon repairs. As guests, they might be able to sleep in a barn or in the house and get a few provisions before starting on the way. He did that often when travelling on his own. He made a few friends that way. People remembered him. His likeability paid off.

The farther they got, the more Rebecca's panic settled down. She had quiet time to think. Being on the road, going to a strange new place, was a leap into an unknown world. She had not really been so clever, but there is no way she could have expected what was coming. If she had been able to bring Jenny and the babies, that would have meant they had even more to contend with. A black nanny like Jenny would have caused Sir John to get the slave catchers after them. There was no sign of people following yet. Maybe they got tired of her and were just as glad to have her gone. Maybe now they'll just leave her alone.

Whatever made Mr. Turner decide to help, it was a blessing. She doubted that she would have known how to talk to people. His smile and easy manner worked like magic. She would have been terrified and led trackers straight to them. The boys took to Turner in a surprising way. She too was trusting him.

She started to talk to him more about what was on her mind. "Do you think they even care now that they are rid of me. They may be glad I'm gone. I know I was not easy to have around. Good riddance! Not worth going after!"

She was surprised when he started laughing like she just said the funniest thing. "You think that, do you. You out foxed an old fox. You think he'll let you get away with that? If you'd been a man, that would be worth fighting over. Southern gentlemen believe in one thing above all others - honor. They can't stand someone telling them they're wrong. No woman can be smarter. Makes them look weak."

"They wouldn't have any idea where we went," she protested. "We haven't seen any signs that they are following."

He didn't want this to seem hopeless, but she needed to understand what was likely to happen. "You could have run off on your own but think about the boys. You married Old Sir John's oldest son. You do understand what that means. Now that his son passed, his oldest son is the next in line."

"Delila would not agree. She would put her boy James in charge. She doesn't want it any other way."

"But Old John can't give up just like that. That man can't lose. He wants Abe back because he wants to save face. He can't let that happen. Somebody has to pay. Rebecca, I'm afraid that person is going to be me. He'd love to hang me."

"No, it's my doing. I'm the one who is the cause!"

Turner dipped his head and looked into her eyes. "Letting you be the problem is putting a stain on his house. When he comes around to it there will be a story that I'm the one who tainted your judgement and got you to take off. You are a good-looking woman. Why wouldn't I?"

Her head snapped back, like she'd just been whipped across the face. "I am so sorry. I didn't mean to cause this for you. You have saved us. I prayed for an angel, and there you were."

"Don't know that any one has ever called me an angel, but we won't get caught. I have skills and know how to get this done. We are ahead, but they will be on horseback. I know where you can get your new start, and they haven't a clue. We've done great so far."

"I was only thinking about myself. I wanted my boys with me. I am putting people I care about in danger."

"We both knew what was going to happen to you if you just let it go where it was headed. You'd be with a new husband known to beat wives into submission. Your children wouldn't all be welcome with the Spencers. I guarantee they would not keep all of them. Four is a lot of somebody else's babies to raise. You may try to do the most loving thing you can, but lady, nothing is perfect. All of life is dangerous. We just do the best we can."

"You have a way of saying things Mr. Turner. Did you mean that part about me being good-looking?" she asked.

"Well, that's pretty obvious for anyone to see. Why did you think those women didn't like you?" he smiled.

She pondered this a bit. "I thought I was ignorant, and they knew I was beneath them."

Mr. Turner focused back on the road. "I'm sure that's what they wanted you to believe. They just couldn't deal with another woman that much smarter, so they tried to take you down any way they could."

They rode for a bit in silence, then he commented, "We'll be in Charleston soon. We can get anything you might be needing. Maybe find a place to stay that has beds with sheets. The boys can get cleaned up."

When they got up and around the next day, shopping for supplies, Rebecca's breath stopped. She quickly left the store to find Turner and the boys. He had already seen what she saw. One of Old Sir John's hands was in this town with them. He would head back to the plantation and remove all doubt about the direction they had travelled. Rebecca was told to go back to buy little candies for Abraham and Isaac. The boys thought this was a great idea. While there she was to tell them in front of the shopkeepers that this was their treat to eat on the way to Parkersburg. Mr. Turner picked up the horses and wagon from the stable and asked the best road to take for Parkersburg.

They took off to the north. Nobody in the town had any hint they were going to turn west and go to Huntington where a person could find passage on the Ohio River. They needed to stay in the lead as long as possible. Now they were working as a team.

Installment 9

It was so much easier going from Charleston to Huntington, different from the hill country. No more threatening drops and constant worry, wondering if, when, and where pursuers would track them from Patrick County, Virginia. Mr. Turner explained that they would soon ride on a wide river and go farther west than they had ever been before. That sounded hopeful to Rebecca. She encouraged the boys to keep watch for new finds along the way and add to the rock collections. This part of the trip was different, going faster. The air even smelled different. The road was smoother, but people looked rougher to her. Life on a southern plantation was far behind them.

The closer they got to Huntington, the more excited Turner seemed to be. He was well known on the river front. He wanted to look for Karl and Otto Fischer. They ran a flatboat business. He had helped with that for a few months. When he left to go farther east, they had the boat with a shed for passengers to be under cover and a broad deck for livestock and merchandise. The brothers liked him as an extra hand for poling, going upriver after the less strenuous ride down.

They could take the wheels off a wagon, lay them flat, and set the wagon bed on that.

He left Rebecca with the children and wagon to go down the bank looking for Papa Walter. When he saw the old man fishing off a dock, he quickly covered the distance and was greeted with a hug and slap on the back. "Sam, look at you. It's been a while! What are you doing back here with us? I can find you a job here if you want it."

"Walter it's so good to see you. How is everybody?"

"The boys are running the boat, if that's what you're asking. Got Karl's son, Paul, helping too. Your name comes up a lot."

"I want to be a paying customer if you got room. I'm escorting a lady and her children." He pointed to Rebecca and the boys at the top of the rise. "We need to go down river a piece with a few horses and a wagon. Is the boat out right now?"

"The boys should be back in Huntington in a couple days, we've got a few other things booked, but there will be room for you. You'll be really pleased. They upgraded the accommodations for passengers. The shed doesn't leak so in bad weather."

"First class! I'd expect nothing less from the Fischers!" Turner went back to Rebecca to share the good news. Good and maybe not so good. He could tell them that they would be on their way in a couple of days, but this was also going to cost.

They hadn't had much travel expense, but that was going to end. They would need to check into Auntie French's boarding house and stable the horses with the wagon. There was a conference about finances. He needed to explain that it was time to think about what from the wagon could be sold or traded. He had spent money that was supposed to be used for buying horses back in Virginia, and he worked for some of their provisions, but expenses are about to change. He would try to leave as much as he could for her homesteading. Rebecca responded that she was already expecting to trade with the tobacco bundles, the jewelry, and some of the fancy stuff; but she trusted him to make the best deals he could. They just had to be out of the reach of plantation agents. When they were finally safe, it would be like starting over.

"I'm sure you can take care of things, Lady. I will at least get you settled. This may be tough. We aren't there yet"

"Do what you need to do. I am so grateful for your help," she said.

Once they were settled in, the boys wanted to go down to watch the water, so the adults followed a bit behind. "I've heard people calling you 'Sam,'" she gave him a quizzing look.

"Well, that's my name."

"I've only heard you called Mr. Turner," she responded.

"Because that's all they called me back at the Spencer farm. I sort of lived here for a while, when I was younger. I came through here maybe a year ago." That was all he said.

"Hmm," she thought as they walked along. They noticed a circle of boys kneeling in the dirt as Abraham and Isaac slowed up to watch what they were doing. The town boys had drawn a circle in the dirt and put a pile of little round marbles made of a rock wrapped in clay in the center. Taking turns rolling a shooter marble into the circle, the aim was to see how many of the targets from the center would be knocked out of the circle. Each player had a different technique for making the shot. At the start of a new round, the guests were invited to borrow a shooter and see how they did. The beginners didn't do so well, but they were hooked.

Later that evening, the Spencer boys were each rolling spheres from the river clay to let them dry and become solid. They explained the rules for the new game.

Mr. Turner smiled and said they had just learned a really old game. "There's a story about a king who went off to war and was gone a long, long time. Men came from all over to court the king's wife, thinking they might rule the kingdom if she married them. She stalled, thinking surely her husband would return. While they waited around for her to make up her mind, they played games, something like this, to pass the time."

"That's an old story, Mr. Turner?" asked Abraham.

"Sure is," he answered. "It's about a time when the Greeks had heroes that went off to great battles."

"Mama, those guys had tin buckets they kept the marbles in," said Isaac. "They said they asked down at the diner to see if they had old lard tins they wanted to get rid of. Can we do that too?"

"We could keep our rock collections in there too," his brother added.

"Don't see why you can't ask, if that's OK with your mom. I'd go with them," offered Turner.

After the boys settled in to sleep, Rebecca had a chance to ask, "How do you know about the stories from the Odyssey? First, I learn your given name is Sam, and now I see you know Greek classics."

"I guess there's a lot about me you don't know," he answered. "The Odyssey is full of good stories. Every kid who likes adventure should know them."

The Fischer flatboat returned just as Walter said. Loading in the other passengers, the merchandise, and livestock took a while. The brothers looked to Sam like a long, lost brother. They talked about old times. Rebecca was pleased to see another mother with little ones who would ride with her in the shed; but when they were ready to shove off, she started to worry about the baby the lady kept bundled in her arms. The little one had a persistent cough and looked like it had a fever. She let Turner know that she would like him to help watch the boys. Maybe it would be good if they could sit out of the shed as much as possible.

When they moved to the middle of the current and picked up speed, Abraham came to get the attention of his mother. "Mama, I saw Grandpa."

"No, Abe, Grandpa is back at the farm," she answered. Then she looked over at the bank. By the southern shore was Old Sir John. James was riding up to join him with Uncle Lewis and Uncle Alex. How could they have caught up so quickly? The river started carrying her swiftly downstream. When she told Turner, he had a look of concern; but she could tell he already had a plan.

They got off the flatboat at Cincinnati and gave the Fischer crew a hearty farewell. The wagon was hitched quickly to the team, and Turner took them to a lovely farmstead north of the town. No time to look around.

A boy out in the yard spotted them and ran up to see what they wanted. Turner was completely at ease as he quizzed the child. "Would this still be the Jack and Berta Wagner place? You can tell them Sam Turner is here to see them."

The boy spun around and raced back toward the front door. Just that fast, a woman in a house dress came running out to meet them. "Is that you Sam Turner? I can't wait to tell Jack you are here!" Rebecca and her boys watched as the reunion commenced.

Jack and Sam were slapping each other on the back and throwing friendly punches with questions flying back and forth. Sam explained what his predicament was; and Jack said, "You've come the right place. I can help you make this happen. Anything for a brother!"

Berta welcomed the passengers into the house. Rebecca knew that she wouldn't be made to feel more at home if she'd gotten to Adaline's. All the kids treated both women like the "mom." While they worked together getting ready for a supper, Berta shared that a flu of some sort just went through Cincinnati, and that was really hard on children. Both of Berta's children came down with it, but she was one of the fortunate mothers who didn't lose a little one. Rebecca told about Turner guiding her away from the people who hated her on the farm and over the mountains. The young widow's father-in-law had chased them all the way from Virginia. He seemed determined not to give up. She hadn't shared like this with anybody, not even Jenny.

As it turns out, Jack's parents raised Sam as one of their own after his parents died. No wonder the men acted like pups from the same litter. The guys were planning together and going back into Cincinnati tomorrow. Abraham and Isaac were in heaven with new playmates who included them automatically.

When Jack and Sam returned the next day, they now drove a larger covered wagon with a new team of oxen. They had found a wagon train going west at the start of next week. The trail boss would include Sam and "his family" in their caravan. Everyone had to get ready. But Rebecca had bad news that she knew she had to share about the departure. Her heart was sinking.

Tenth Installment

Sam described his new plan for throwing the men from the plantation off their trail. Over the mountains, across western Virginia and onto the Ohio River, Rebecca and the boys had been pursued by men on horseback who never gave up. At the start she had convinced people she wanted a week to visit her family in the Virginia hills, but she then went west. When the fugitives got to Charleston, they spread the word that they were heading north to Parkersburg and then went west to Huntington on the Ohio River. Sam wanted to keep his promise to get her to new territory. He was determined that she could start that new life.

After the ride down the river, they got off in Cincinnati and headed north to Jack and Berta Wagner's. He decided it was time to get serious about disguise. Up to now he told people he was hired by a Virginia landowner, escorting a widowed daughter-in-law and her boys to see her relatives. Which was true, sort of. They left out the part that if she returned, she would be doomed to a brutal, arranged marriage. She had taken the chance to run with two of the children and convinced Sam Turner to give up working for Sir John Spencer and be her guide. Actually, he had volunteered.

They had been traveling alone with a small, covered wagon, Sam's horse tied alongside. If they changed to a wagon train, they would be hiding in the middle of all the other people going the same direction. Old Sir John had been stubborn. The followers would think the wayward family had vanished. Turner was last seen being carried away on the river from Huntington. When would Sir John give up trying to prove he was the master and head back to Virginia? Jack Wagner and Sam thought this wagon train plan was great. They made all the arrangements, then came back to the Wagner farm to show Rebecca.

The men wanted her to be excited. She had to see how this could all work, but she hesitated. Had they overstepped? Rebecca and Sam had been working as a team with the boys. Maybe this was too much of a change when she didn't even know it was coming. Did she not like the "family" part. He only wanted to get her to the Wisconsin Territory without having those relatives know where she was. He would love to see her get that new life. He had promised her and promised himself that he would get this done. It felt like being noble, doing something good.

"What's wrong?" he asked. "I know oxen aren't as smart as the horses were, but they're easy to handle. A bigger wagon will be more comfortable, maybe we'll find more things to bring for your new place. The 'family' part? That will make us fit in with the rest of the folks in the train. Other people don't have to know any better. Don't you like it?"

"Sam, it's a good plan. I would love to have it work." She was trying not to sound ungrateful. "But we need to be watching Isaac. After the ride down the river and that other family bringing a sick baby, I didn't want my boys to catch it. Isaac spent too much time up close to them. What if he picked up something he hasn't been around before."

"Maybe it will be nothing, honey," said Berta. "We can watch him to see if he starts to run a fever or gets a cough." She had just nursed her own children through the latest season of flu and understood Rebecca's concern. Rebecca had great respect for Berta's judgement. Many families lost babies in that flu. Berta got all the Wagner children through, and they were now mostly fine.

"Come on," encouraged Sam. "Give this a look. Jack thinks that the Spencer men won't know where we got off the raft. If they do figure that out, we were out of town so fast, nobody will know where we went after Cincinnati. The idea of a wagon train changes everything. We won't look the same."

As they all inspected the sturdy new wagon, everyone agreed the plan seemed very good. Berta said that it would help if Rebecca looked more the part of a pioneer wife. The two women took an empty feed sack to make into a proper frontier dress. There weren't any frills or soft materials, but the family would look more like they belonged in with the other families on the trail. It was starting to get exciting. Almost there!

Rebecca felt freer here in Ohio than she had in years. The Wagners laughed more and shared interesting stories. Many of those stories were about Sam Turner growing up. He took it all with his usual smile but said there may be some exaggeration and inventing. The children became one happy tribe until little Isaac started coughing with the start of a headache. Berta went into action as the supreme caregiver. She said this was just how that flu started, and they should expect him to run a fever. Some children took more than two weeks before they were on the mend. Getting better only happened with a lot of rest, a chest plaster, her special syrup, some warm broth, and calm. There were too many fresh markers in the cemetery not to take this seriously.

Making the deadline for the wagon train lineup and departure meant Rebecca and Sam should head out the next day. Rebecca could not risk one of her little ones. She left the two babies with Jenny back at the plantation. It felt like her family was crumbling. She and Berta sat together in silence on the porch while the men finished caring for the animals for the evening.

Berta began what she needed to say. "I suppose you know that Sam Turner is a very special man. Jake's family took him when he was just school age. He was good at everything and so likeable. The other kids just had to be his friend. Those that challenged him usually found themselves up a creek."

"I know Sam's one of a kind. He has been so good to us. We wouldn't be here without him," responded Rebecca.

Berta had not yet made her point. "There were a lot of girls who wanted to tie him down when we were all younger. But things have changed in him now. Taking care of you is very important to him. Be very careful. Please don't do something that gets him killed. You need to take care of him too."

"Oh Berta. This is all too much for me. I know the wagon train will make it just that much more certain that he doesn't have to face off with the Spencer men. But how can I lose another baby. Samuel and Sissy are back in Virginia with a Mammy. Abe and Isaac are all I have now." There was a mother's pain in her voice.

"I promise you, if you let me take care of Isaac, we will do everything we can to get him back to you. Sam told Jake where he thinks you can get settled. I will make sure your little guy is better as soon as possible. The flu is cruel. I know families who had six kids but lost every one of them last month. There is no mercy in too many of life's choices."

"How can I just leave Isaac?"

"You would be leaving him with me. That's different. I have to believe that you will take care of Sam. You are like my sister. Can we do any less?"

The women sat in silence for a while. Then Rebecca turned to Berta with a big hug and said, "Thank you."

The next morning Rebecca sat with Isaac and told him that he had a very important job. He had to do everything Berta said so he would get well. When they were ready, Jake and Berta would bring him to catch up with his brother. They would be fixing a new home in the territory and have a place for him. Abe made sure that Isaac had his tin of marbles and rocks. He also left his own best rock with his little brother. This was not the happy send off they had wanted, but Sam got everyone to their spot in the line-up.

It felt safer to follow the lead of a wagon master with fourteen other wagons. Like a small town moving along old Indian trails, this was security, but also monotony. The farther they went, the less likely that they would see any more of the Spencer group. Nobody on the train acted like they were anything special, and that was just fine. The mind had a chance to look at different things. Sam Turner was planning how exactly to start a fresh homestead. Rebecca should feel like she found her home. He wondered, would there be enough time to get a first crop of "three sisters" before the season changed? A ring of corn would be support for climbing beans. The pumpkins and squash would go out across the ground. Wild game and fish in the pot would be great.

Rebecca, however, spent her time in quiet. Down deep in her soul as she began to face how life had gone since that ride from the hills to the Spencer farm as a new bride. Mr. Turner figured she had a lot to ponder and would be worried about Isaac. Some women never recovered from lost children. Some who pushed ahead wore that tired warrior look for the rest of their life. He wanted to see her spirit mended and was willing to give it time.

She had questions about life to think through. How did life go terribly wrong after marrying Trip? Was she too young, believing in fairy stories like a little girl? Why was it such a shock when she was treated like an ignorant intruder? She really did learn their excellent manners and all those skills of "good breeding." It didn't matter. She was still treated as a threat who was not worthy. To be fair, she had seen them as empty-headed, useless, and mean-spirited. Her mother-in-law probably knew that. But Rebecca was never good at hiding the fact that she looked down on a "lady" who ordered other people to do things she should be doing for herself. Comfort for a few meant misery or fear or both for the many. They had to build a pile of lies to live with it all. Maybe they were right. She did not fit in.

Life had been so easy with Mama and Daddy. Everyone was part of the team and pulled together. The women on the plantation had traded away a real life for pretty things and what they thought was protection. She wanted the children back, but losing a piece of your heart was the curse of being a woman. She wanted a world where people would not be always pushing to be the top of the heap. She wanted people she could appreciate, and who valued her in return. She wanted to belong to people like that. Some things felt good. She loved the Wagners. A soft thought occurred to her, she felt good about Sam Turner.

Gradually the Turner family joined with neighbors in the circle of wagons for the evening. The progress was slower now than when they were on horseback, but it was steady and there were no wrong turns. Sam broke the ice with all the strangers who had a common goal of leaving the past behind to go west. Each had personal reasons for making the trip, but in a sense they all had the same reason. They were making a new start. Most planned to farm, but there was also a mix of skills. There was a preacher who had church for them on the trail. One gentleman wanted to set up a trading post. Another was set on offering service in blacksmithing.

On the way back to their wagon, Abe was still singing a catchy song he learned about a farmer. That farmer had all kinds of animals. Abraham wanted their new place to have a cow and a dog and a cat and a horse and chickens and ducks. Rebecca and Sam laughed and said that could be their goal. They would have to see about all that.

When they were retiring for the night, Rebecca and Sam had time to talk. They talked about places they'd been and people they knew. They talked about the life a person could have in the territory. One night Rebecca said, "You know, one of my babies in Virginia is named Samuel. Samuel Washington Spencer."

"I think I knew that," was the reply.

"He is a wonderful boy. He stayed with Jenny. I hope she still has him. She was the only Mammy he ever knew. Sometimes we called him Sammy." She looked him straight in the eyes, "You are pretty special too, Sam Turner. I couldn't be here without you. I see that now."

"So, you are grateful? Is that all?" He waited for her answer.

"Oh, no Sam Turner. Much, much more than that," Rebecca responded.

"I'd be honored if we would make it official. Please say yes." The love in Sam eyes melted her into his arms.

Mr. and Mrs. Turner left the rest of the wagon train after crossing the Mississippi River into Missouri. They then went north and entered the Wisconsin Territory at the far southeastern corner. They settled in what is now called Pittsburg beside the Des Moines River in Iowa. They later moved upstream to the town of Leando.

The family caring for Isaac was not able to find them when they were ready to migrate out west. They kept travelling on to Kansas. Years later, one of Isaac's sons did come back in search of his Spencer relatives and spent time with Abraham. Particulars about the family story follow in the epilogue.

Epilogue

As a little bit of historical fiction, a person might wonder how much is history and how much is fiction. Good question. The year I went through the family letters, clippings, and attempts at genealogies, I was finally able to put together which episodes went with which generations of the many branches on my family tree. Descriptions about Rebecca Akers Spencer Turner were attention-getting and would have been told with eyes just a little wider and a nervous laugh. Putting it politely, she had stronger feelings and more energy than a southern woman in the early eighteen hundreds should have had. My own mother was known to add, "Those Spencers thought they were better than anybody else."

When Rebecca was engaged to the oldest son of a plantation owner, she ruined their formal wedding plans. She was at her own home, scrubbing the floors barefoot when both her intended and the circuit preacher stopped by. She decided to have the wedding then and there. Her new in-laws were not happy.

She moved to the plantation, and the couple quickly had four children. Then her husband died. He was described as "sickly." All of this happened when she was a teenager according to the stories.

While she was in Virginia she was given some lovely earrings for pierced ears. They featured metal work and included a gold coin. Later, she was able to give them to her daughter-in-law, Elizabeth Green Spencer, Samuel's wife. Elizabeth promised to give these earrings to the first granddaughter to be named after her. The girl who probably should have received them was not trusted by Elizabeth. They were family keepsakes. Elizabeth wanted them to be kept in family. Problem was that nobody in that generation wanted to go through the risky procedure of getting their ears pierced. The heirloom jewelry was thought to be worth a lot of money, and Elizabeth wanted them to be worn, not sold. According to a letter from Aunt Margaret, there was a "row" on the day of her funeral when the question came up as to who would get the earrings. Bessie Mae Spencer Michael settled the argument. She buried her mother and earrings too! I hope nobody dug her up looking for them. The only picture I have of Rebecca is not very flattering. She is with Sam Turner and posed for a photographer. She looked like a fierce general after many battles. She is extremely well dressed and has dangling earrings.

She did not get along with her in-laws on a regular basis. Once when she was so angry she turned their two prized stallions into the same corral. The two engaged in mortal combat, and the Spencer family lost the two valuable animals. There was no explanation about what led up to that horrifying act.

Rebecca decided to run away with a "horse trader," Sam Turner. They took off with the two oldest children, Abraham and Isaac. Their route from the big house took them through the plantation's corn field. The men of the plantation chased them relentlessly. While riding down Ohio River, the fleeing couple saw the pursuers on the bank.

In Ohio, the youngest child became sick with fever and was left behind with another family. That family tried to find the Turner family when they also migrated west. They were not able locate Isaac's mother, so they kept travelling. They settled in Kansas; and the boy, Isaac Spencer, grew to be a man there. His own child later came back to Iowa and stayed for a time with Abraham in southeast Iowa.

There were two babies left behind on the plantation. Samuel was the older one, and he joined his mother in Iowa when he was an older teen. He is my great, great grandfather. My grandmother, Willa May Michael Stump was interviewed by one of the cousins; and I have a recording of that conversation. Her comments about her grandfather gave me little bit of information.

She told her interviewer that Samuel was raised by the Spencer family on a plantation. He knew he had a baby sister but couldn't remember her name. She was given to an aunt from "York State," an early name for the Massachusetts area. Samuel was raised by a black Mammy who "loved him dearly, and he loved her." He left Virginia when his caregiver either died, was reassigned, or sold. He did not want to fight in the war between the states because Iowa was sending troops to support the north. He was concerned that he would be asked to fight his relatives. Instead, he signed on as a guard for a wagon train going to California. After the war was over, he was told that many of his people died, and the men lost the plantation. He had been given an education growing up, and his own children also had this opportunity, including the girls. His daughter Bessie Mae met her future husband, Will Michael, when she was teaching in Van Buren County. I have a picture of her with her students in front of the schoolhouse.

There is a family Bible from Ohio that has contrary information. It states that Samuel Spencer was born there. This does not match anything else that people in the family, from Rebecca on down, would tell about my Grandma Willa Michael Stump's grandfather. Willa was the oldest child of Bessie Mae Spencer Michael, Samuel's daughter. Willa had spoken directly to her grandfather before he died when she was a teenager.

Once in the interview with Grandma Stump, she mentioned that Samuel was raised on the plantation of Old Sir John. So I looked on https://ancestors.familysearch.org to see if I could find a John Spencer in Virginia who could have had a son old enough to get married in the 1830's.

There was only one. He lived in Henry County, Virginia. That county was split in two eventually and became Patrick and Henry Counties, just north of Franklin County where I found Daniel Akers who was married to a Rebecca. Their family included a daughter, also named Rebecca, who would be about the right age.

The man I found on the web, John R. Spencer II, was problematic. His family tree had a gaping hole. Most men of the time married in their twenties. For him there was an empty space until almost age forty, when wife Delilah was shown as the mother of a line of little girls. Finally, they had a boy named James in 1833. There was no boy named John Spencer III. It was like an earlier wife and possible children had been erased.

John II's father, John R. Spencer I, also lived in colonial Virginia. John R. Spencer II was his second son. The first son was William R. Cyres Spencer III. That was such an unusual name that I dug a little deeper and found William Robert Spencer (d. 1834), an English poet and wit from the Spencer family. William Robert had 6 children. Two of his sons were Anglican Bishops, one in Newfoundland and Jamaica and the other in India. The "Cyres" is sometimes used as a surname, and its meaning can be "highly intelligent." He was born in Windsor Castle, and he had a position as Commissioner of Stamps; but his profession seemed to be 'very popular celebrity.' A book of his writings and an introductory biography was republished in 2010.

So, if the colonial Spencer family was tied to the Anglican Church of England, having a wedding performed by a Methodist circuit preacher would not have pleased them at all! Intrigue and scheming for position was typical in many who valued wealth and respectability. (Ironic, huh!) Most of the stories told about Rebecca were negative and seemed to tell only half the story. I wondered how someone with any compassion would be provoked to destroy valuable animals. Why would someone make a run with little children in tow? This didn't seem like an impulsive, romantic infatuation, but would need a strategic plan. And how could she outrun men on horseback who were intent on catching up? Why would a mother who was trying to keep her children, leave one behind when the child was sick? Why would children later seek a mother who carelessly abandoned them? If these things actually happened, there must have been another side to Rebecca that was worth thinking about. She did remarkable, unladylike things.

So, what is "history?" Where does something have to be written to be judged as truth? Isn't a lot of history actually only "his-story?" What is written here is more like "her-story."

Geography and History of Iowa

What is today's state of Iowa was part of the Louisiana Purchase, which was later divided into territories. The Wisconsin Territory, including Iowa, was opened for settlement June 1, 1833. The land was already home to many groups of people who had developed patterns of commerce and land use that didn't match the expectations of the new people who were moving in. Before the 1830's there were European explorers, fur trappers, and traders who already moved through, but people intending to settle and enforce their own culture was something new.

The Des Moines River flowed into the Mississippi at the town of Keokuk. The rivers were the highways for movement of goods and people. It was convenient to settle on the banks of the rivers. The vegetation right up to the water helped hold the moving water into deep channels, deep enough that eventually steamboats were able to move about. Bentonsport, for instance, got its name because it was a port, a place to dock. Across the Des Moines River from today's Selma in the northwest corner of Van Buren County was a thriving distillery and trading post. This settlement, named Black Hawk, was a common departure point for wagon trains going west.

Map of Van Buren County, Iowa

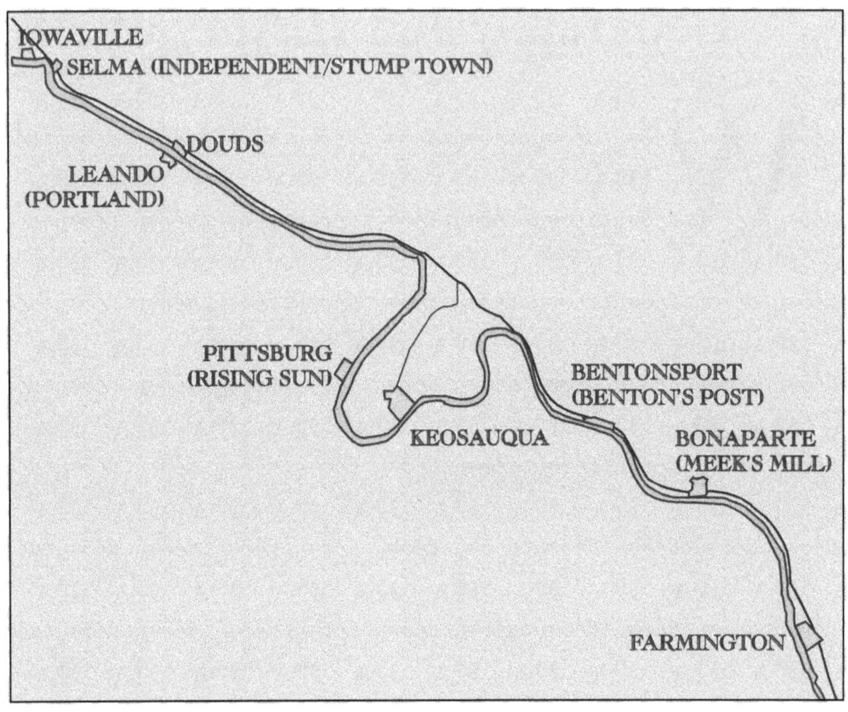

The Des Moines River runs diagonally, from northwest to southeast.

Note: Iowaville, which no longer exists, was the Indian settlement where Chief Blackhawk made his last home. The Iowaville Cemetary on the hill is just north of where the Indians lived.

Rebecca Akers Spencer Turner with Sam Turner, date unknown.

www.ingramcontent.com/pod-product-compliance
Lightning Source LLC
Chambersburg PA
CBHW040913010826
48978CB00013BB/1275